THE VERY BEST BED

Rebekah Raye

TILBURY HOUSE PUBLISHERS

The little gray squirrel
was so busy finding nuts and seeds
to store away for the winter
that he hadn't noticed
it was getting cold and dark.
He needed to find a cozy bed
for the night.

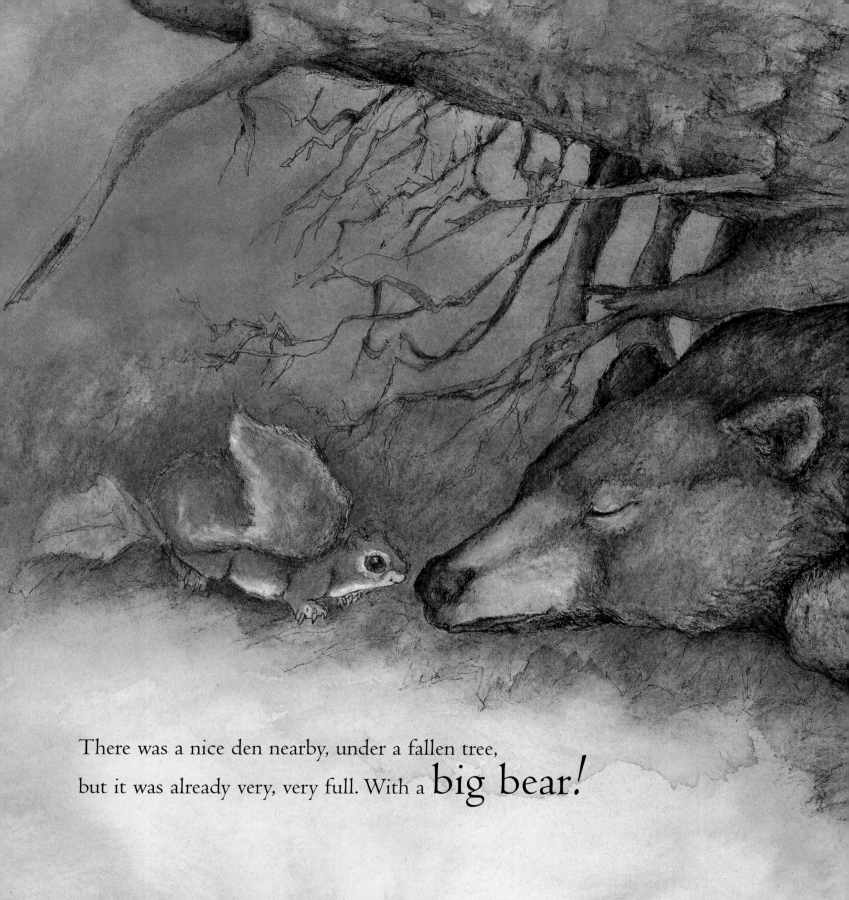

There was a nice den nearby, under a fallen tree,
but it was already very, very full. With a big bear!

Could he find a nest up in the old pine tree?

But then he heard the sound of a barred owl hooting.

It sounded like:

WHO COOKS FOR YOUUUUU ALLLLLLL...?

The owl was just waking up.

Soon he would start hunting in the moonlight.

The squirrel jumped up onto a great pile of rocks.

There was a safe little cave there, but when he peeked inside

he saw a red fox, snuggled up with his warm bushy tail.

What if the fox woke up hungry, too?

It might be safer up
in the tall maple tree, so
up he climbed.

up,

up,

A family of bats was hanging upside
down from the branches. The squirrel
tried it, but it made his head ache.
Ouch!

With a big **jump**,
the squirrel leaped to a nearby apple tree.

Down below he saw a trail of nibbled apples.

They looked delicious. Two deer rested there.

It would be warm to snuggle between them,

but they woke up and started to move away.

Deer only sleep for a few hours at a time.

hop,

He followed a cottontail rabbit hop,   hopping towards a group of thick, young spruce trees. It was heading for a small hollow in the grass, lined with leaves. What a perfect place to sleep! Too bad it was only big enough for one rabbit.

Down by the water's edge,
the squirrel saw ducks and geese
sleeping on rafts of reeds and cattails.
The gentle waves rocked them back and forth.
But the squirrel didn't want to get his own little feet wet.

A ripple of water caught his eye.

He watched two seals bobbing upright

and a harbor porpoise gently rolling

on the surface of the water.

It looked like they didn't mind sleeping in the water at all.

Imagine that!

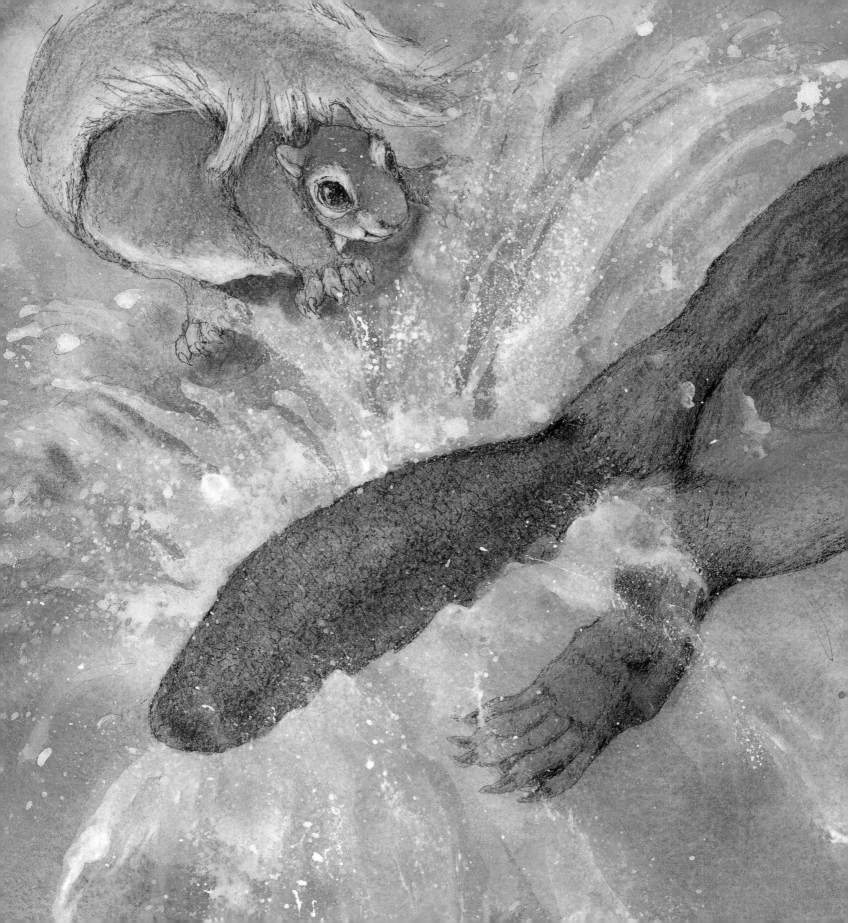

At the pond on his way back
to the woods, the squirrel
saw a big beaver slap
his flat tail on the water
and dive down into his lodge
in the middle of the pond.
But the squirrel certainly did not want to get his
fluffy tail wet. A wet tail was just as bad as wet feet!

The sky was getting darker, but the squirrel noticed a tiny hole at the base

of an oak tree. He peeked inside and saw a chipmunk sleeping on a bed of

leaves and grass. There were lots of seeds nearby in case he woke up hungry.

It looked very, very cozy—especially with a snack so handy—but there

wasn't quite enough room for a squirrel, too!

So the squirrel began
to climb higher up the oak tree.
He saw a mama raccoon resting on
a branch next to a bigger hole in the tree.
But when he looked inside, there was a nest
full of raccoon babies. It didn't look like they
would be going to sleep anytime soon!

The squirrel kept climbing

higher.

and

higher

and

higher

And there, sheltered under a branch,

was an empty woodpecker's nest.

Quick as a flash, the squirrel scampered

down

the

tree

and gathered some grass and moss and leaves.

Then he made
the very best bed
there ever was.
He curled up under
his fluffy tail
and slept
and slept
and slept. All night long!

Do YOU think the squirrel
had the very best bed of all?

TILBURY HOUSE, PUBLISHERS
2 Mechanic Street
Gardiner, Maine 04345
800–582–1899 • www.tilburyhouse.com

First hardcover printing: September 2006 • 10 9 8 7 6 5 4 3

Dedication—
For my mother and father, Frankie and Ray, and my son, Seth — RR

Library of Congress Cataloging-in-Publication Data

Raye, Rebekah.
   The very best bed / Rebekah Raye.
      p. cm.
   Summary: A squirrel with his store of seeds and nuts hunts for a
cozy bed but he must search high and low for a spot that is not
already occupied by other animals.
   ISBN-13: 978-0-88448-284-0 (hardcover : alk. paper)
   ISBN-10: 0-88448-284-7 (hardcover : alk. paper)
   [1. Squirrels--Fiction. 2. Beds--Fiction. 3. Animals--Fiction.]
I. Title.
PZ7.R21036Ver 2006
[E]--dc22
                                              2006022568

Designed by Geraldine Millham, Westport, Massachusetts
Printed by Sung In Printing, South Korea